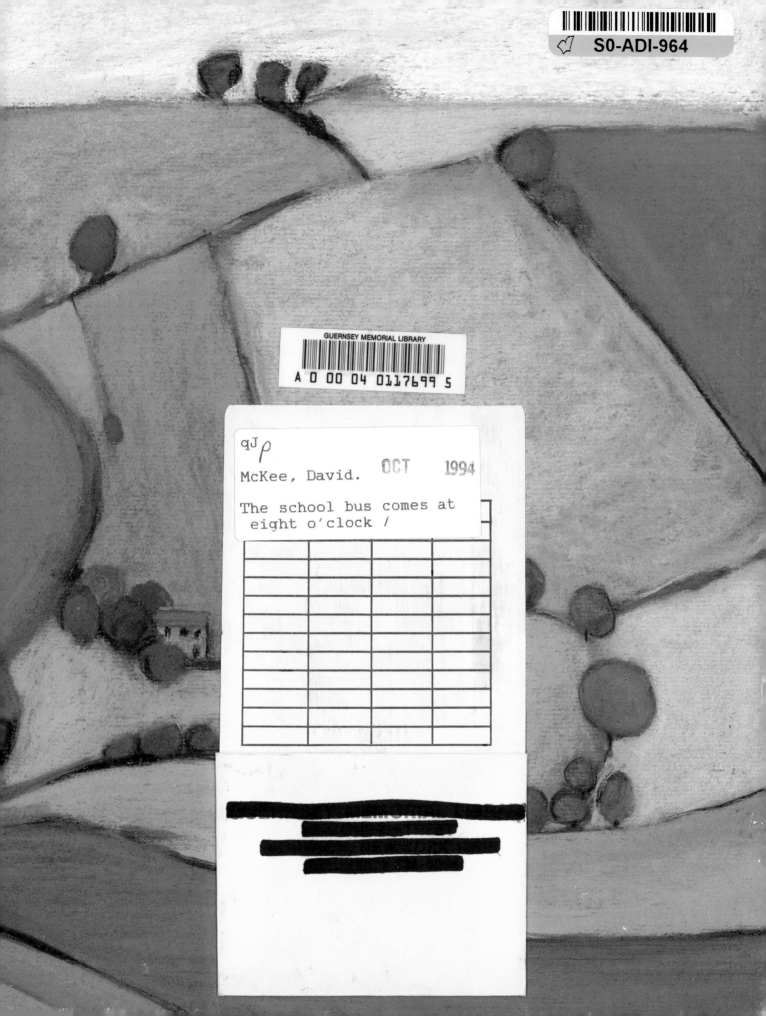

In memory of Andrew Hollingsworth,
a very special bookseller

Text and illustrations © 1994 by David McKee.
All rights reserved.
Printed in Italy.
For information address Hyperion Books for Children,
114 Fifth Avenue, New York, New York 10011.
FIRST EDITION
1 3 5 7 9 10 8 6 4 2

ISBN: 1-56282-662-X/1-56282-663-8 (lib. bdg.)

The artwork for each picture is prepared using pastel.

This book is set in 14-point Caxton Book.

The SCHOOL BUS comes at EIGHT O'CLOCK

DAVID McKEE

HYPERION BOOKS FOR CHILDREN/NEW YORK

It was Jennifer and Eric's first day of school.
They were outside waiting for the school bus with
their parents and their cat, Cleo.

"We know that the school bus comes at eight
o'clock," said Jennifer, "but we don't have a clock to tell
us when eight o'clock *is*."

"Yes," said Eric. "Why don't we have any clocks?"

"Neither your father nor I have ever had much use for
them. Perhaps we do need one now that you two are in
school," said Mrs. Gilbert. "Let's look for one this
weekend."

"Well, it must be eight o'clock because here's the
school bus," said Mr. Gilbert. "Run for it, Eric."

That weekend the Gilbert family went to a flea market. Mrs. Gilbert discovered a beautiful antique grandfather clock.

"This will be perfect!" she said.

They paid for it and loaded it into their pickup truck.

"We'll start it as soon as we get home," said Eric excitedly.

"We can't," said Mrs. Gilbert. "We don't know what time it is. We'll have to wait until Monday morning when the school bus comes at eight o'clock."

On Monday morning when the bus arrived, Mr. Gilbert started the clock. After school, Eric and Jennifer rushed in the house to look at it.

"It's four o'clock now," said Eric. "That means dinner is in two hours, at six o'clock."

"That's right," said Mrs. Gilbert. "And bedtime is two hours after dinner, at eight o'clock."

That night the clock struck every hour. No one slept very well. The next morning both the children got ready for school and watched as the hands on the clock slowly turned to point to eight o'clock.

"Eight o'clock," said Jennifer. "The school bus comes at eight o'clock. Let's go, Eric."

A little while later the children came back in again.

"The bus isn't here yet," said Jennifer.

"Maybe the clock is wrong," said Eric.

"Yes," said Jennifer. "How would we know?"

When the clock showed half past eight the bus finally arrived. "Sorry we are late," the bus driver apologized. "We had a flat tire."

"The clock was right after all!" Eric and Jennifer said together.

"It might not have been and we would never have known," said Mr. Gilbert. He and Mrs. Gilbert waved as the bus drove away.

When they got home from school, Jennifer and Eric
discovered their father had purchased another clock so that
the family would be sure to know what time it was. At first
the two clocks ran together, but gradually there was a slight
difference. At midnight the two clocks chimed separately,
first one and then the other — twenty-four chimes in all.

"I thought one chiming clock was bad," said Jennifer.

"Yes," said Eric. "This is twice as bad as before."

Cleo meowed in agreement.

"We will get used to it," said Mrs. Gilbert.

"I hope so," said Mr. Gilbert.

The next morning, the two clocks didn't tell the same time. Eric and Jennifer argued about which clock was wrong. The school bus waited outside.

Perhaps we should get another clock, Mrs. Gilbert thought to herself. That might help.

Mr. Gilbert bought a clock that day.

"With three clocks we'll know which is wrong," he said. "I'll put it on the mantlepiece."

"I went shopping, too!" said Mrs. Gilbert. "This cuckoo clock will look lovely in the dining room."

"Now we have four clocks," said Mr. Gilbert. "We'll always know what time it is!"

Eric and Jennifer were fascinated by the cuckoo clock.
They watched it as they ate their dinner.
   "Well," said Mrs. Gilbert, "I hope this works."
   Mr. Gilbert was worried. It seemed to him that all four
clocks struck the hour at different times.

After supper, the children played outside for a while.

"It's getting late," Mrs. Gilbert called. "Come in and get ready for bed."

"Not yet. I'm winning," said Jennifer.

"I can still win," said Eric. "I didn't hear the cuckoos yet."

"The cuckoo clock is slow," Mrs. Gilbert replied. "It's time to come in."

At midnight, the whole family was awakened by
thirty-six chimes followed by twelve "cuckoos."
"Four clocks is twice as bad as two!" said Eric.

"How long *will* it take for us to get used to it?" said Jennifer.
"Too long," said Mr. Gilbert.

The next morning Mr. Gilbert announced he was getting rid of the clocks. "We will keep the grandfather clock, but it stays stopped at eight o'clock."

Mrs. Gilbert said, "A fast clock is never right, and a slow clock is never right, but a stopped clock will be right twice a day."

"Yes," said Eric. "It will be right when the school bus comes!"

"And at bedtime," said Jennifer.

And it was, ever after.

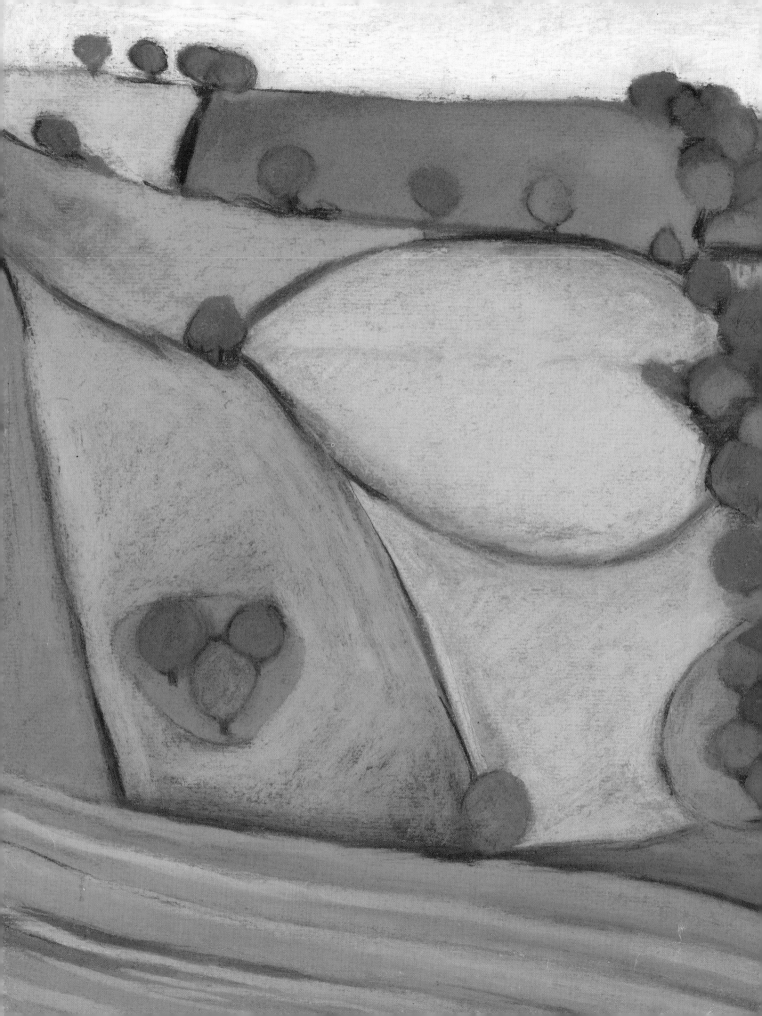